Disney

Who Do You See?

A search-and-find book

By Marilyn Easton

Based on the book THE HUNDRED AND ONE DALMATIANS by Dodie Smith Published by The Viking Press.

The movie THE PRINCESS AND THE FROG Copyright © 2009 Disney, story inspired in part by the book THE FROG PRINCESS by E. D. Baker Copyright © 2002, published by Bloomsbury Publishing, Inc.

Published by Scholastic Australia in 2022.

Scholastic Australia Pty Limited
PO Box 579 Gosford NSW 2250
ABN 11 000 614 577
www.scholastic.com.au

Part of the Scholastic Group
Sydney • Auckland • New York • Toronto • London • Mexico City • New Delhi • Hong Kong • Buenos Aires • Puerto Rico

ISBN 978-1-76120-264-3

Printed in China by RR Donnelley.

Scholastic Australia's policy, in association with RR Donnelley, is to use papers that are renewable and made efficiently from wood grown in responsibly managed forests, so as to minimise its environmental footprint.

10 9 8 7 6 5 4 3 2 22 23 24 25 26 / 2

CHARACTERS

These characters, their friends, and even some villains have gone missing. Can you spot them throughout this book? Be sure to search all over—you never know who you may find!

Moana

A strong-willed explorer, Moana is deeply connected to the ocean and her people.

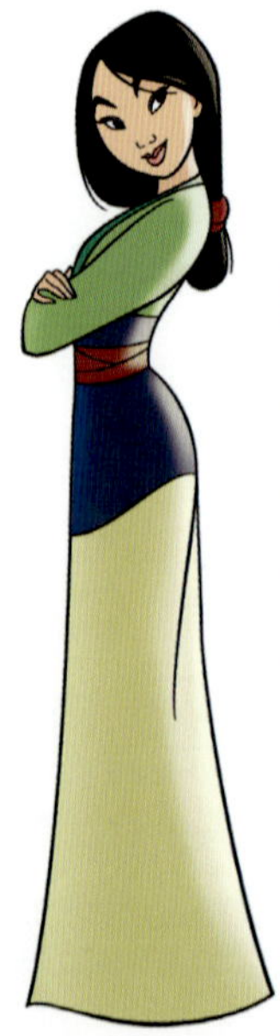

Mulan

By defeating the Huns, brave Mulan brought honour to her family.

Judy Hopps

Officer Hopps is a proud Zootopia police officer with a heart of gold.

Woody

Being a loyal friend and a devoted toy are Woody's top priorities.

Mike Wazowski

At Monsters, Inc., Mike and his best friend, Sulley, work as a team.

Mr. Incredible

Heroic Supers, Mr. Incredible and his family use their special powers to defeat villains.

Nemo

Young and sheltered, Nemo is a clown fish who seeks adventure.

Tiana

Hardworking Princess Tiana believes in herself and follows her dreams.

Simba

The rightful king of the Pride Lands, Simba rules with courage and fairness.

Dumbo

An innocent baby elephant, Dumbo can fly by flapping his big ears.

Lady

Classy, purebred Lady loves Tramp, a charming, collarless mutt.

Pongo

Happy to take care of ninety-nine Dalmatians, Pongo has his paws full.

Jasmine

Outspoken and generous, Princess Jasmine always stands up for herself and others.

Aurora

After overcoming Maleficent's curse, Princess Aurora is dedicated to serving her kingdom.

LOCATIONS

Explore these exciting destinations, from a lively market in Agrabah to a sold-out concert in Zootopia! In each location, you'll discover a unique set of characters to find. Turn to page 34 for even more characters and objects to search for in each scene.

Motunui

China

Zootopia

Second Chance Antiques

Monsters, Inc.

Municiburg

Coral Reef

New Orleans

Pride Rock

The Circus

Tony's Restaurant

London

Agrabah

Princess Aurora's Castle

Motunui

On the island of Motunui, Moana and her people are about to embark on an exciting voyage. Can you find Moana among the villagers? Is shape-shifting Maui in his human form?

China

It's a heroes' celebration parade for the warriors who defeated the Huns. Mulan's friends have joined the parade, but where is Mulan? Can you spot her dog, Little Brother?

Zootopia

Oh, no! Two sloth parents have lost track of their child at an outdoor Gazelle concert. Officers Judy Hopps and Nick Wilde are on the case. Can you spot them among the roaring crowd?

Second Chance Antiques

Inside Second Chance Antiques,
Woody and his friends are trying to
find Bonnie's new favourite toy, Forky.
Can you help them spot him?
Where are Woody and Buzz?

Silver Can

Monsters, Inc.

It's a typical day at Monsters, Inc., until . . . red alert! An item from the human world has contaminated the Scare Floor. Can you spot the source of the outbreak? What are Mike and Sulley doing?

CDA
00132

Municiburg

Boom! Crash! The Underminer's machine is causing chaos in Municiburg. Luckily, the Incredibles family is on the scene, ready to save the day. Can you find Mr. Incredible and Elastigirl? Where is Jack-Jack?

WIX

Coral Reef

It's a bustling morning in the coral reef. Nemo is about to leave for school, but where is he? Finding Nemo may be difficult at first, but if you look hard enough, you'll spot him!

New Orleans

All aboard! Princess Tiana and Prince Naveen are on a riverboat waiting to depart. Can you spot them among the crowd? Is Tiana's best friend, Charlotte LaBouff, on the dock or on the boat?

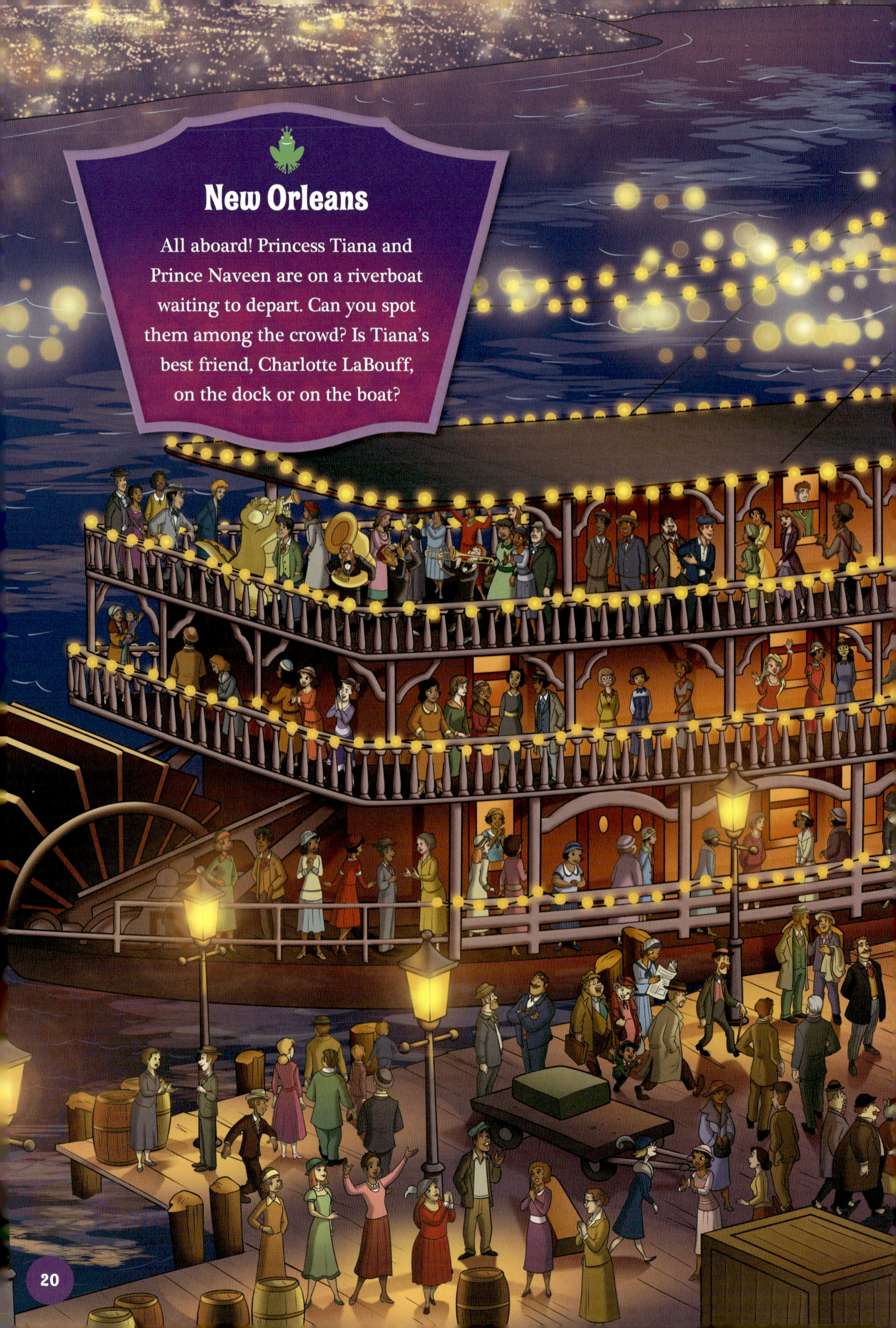

Pride Rock

The animals of the Pride Lands have gathered to hear a special announcement from their lion king, Simba. As Simba addresses the crowd, can you find his friends Timon and Pumbaa?

The Circus

The circus has come to town! The Ringmaster is welcoming visitors inside the tent, but where is Dumbo? Is he performing inside or greeting guests outside? Can you spot Timothy Q. Mouse?

DUMBO
PRIVATE

Tony's Restaurant

Lady and Tramp are heading to a romantic spaghetti dinner at Tony's Restaurant. Their four puppies were supposed to stay home, but they decided to follow their parents instead! Can you find all of the puppies?

TONYS
RESTAURANT
TONY'S

London

Season's greetings! This year, all one hundred and one Dalmatians are spending the holidays together. Is Anita cleaning off a puppy or decorating the tree? Does Pongo have a puppy on his head or on his back?

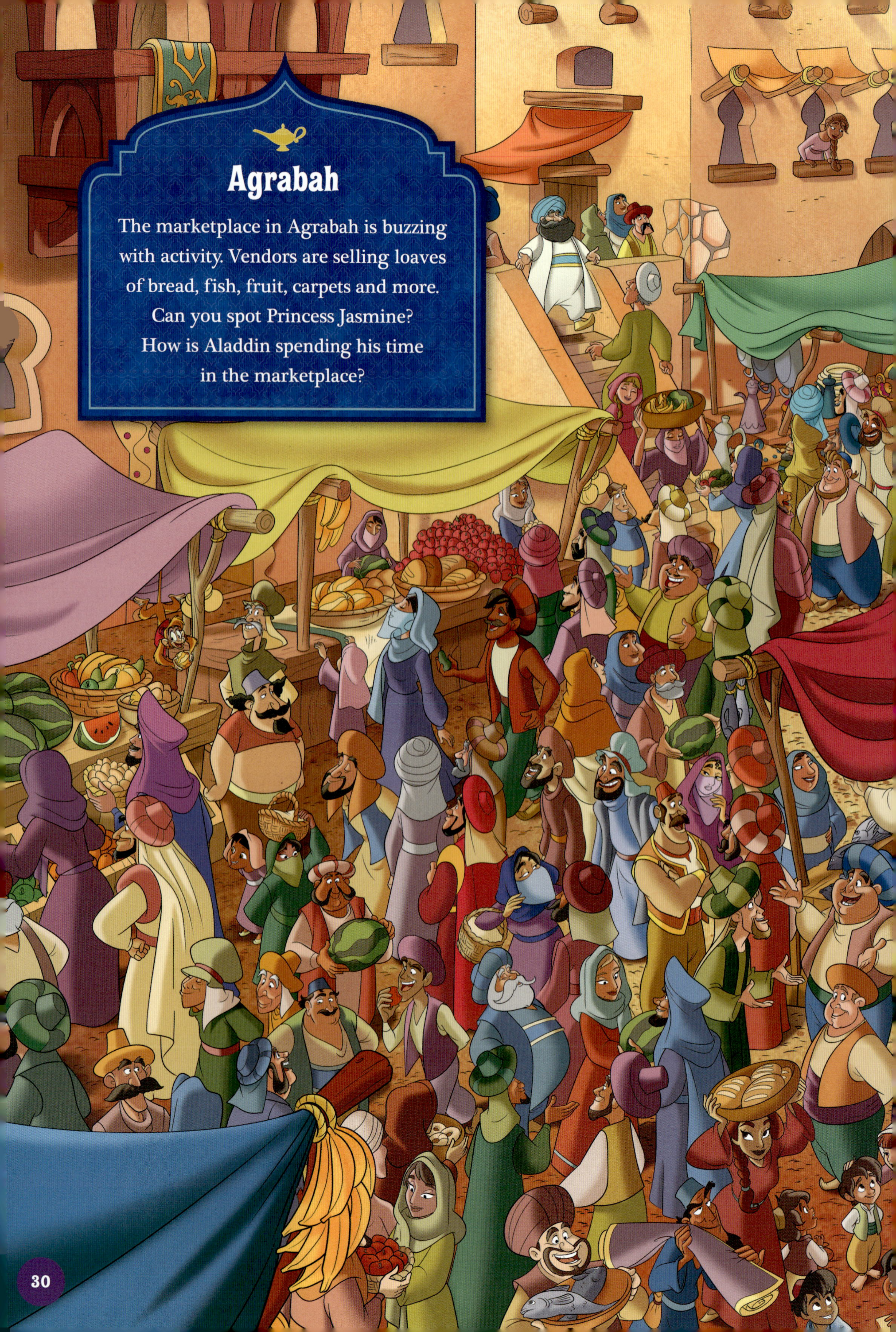

Agrabah

The marketplace in Agrabah is buzzing with activity. Vendors are selling loaves of bread, fish, fruit, carpets and more. Can you spot Princess Jasmine? How is Aladdin spending his time in the marketplace?

Princess Aurora's Castle

It's a royal celebration at Princess Aurora's castle. But where is the princess who was once a sleeping beauty? Is she seated on an elegant throne or standing with her guests? Can you find Prince Phillip?

Look out for these extra characters and objects to search for:

Motunui (pages 6-7)
- Chief Tui
- Sina
- Pua
- Heihei
- Stingray

China (pages 8-9)
- Cri-Kee
- Mushu
- Grandmother Fa
- Fa Zhou
- Fa Li

Zootopia (pages 10-11)
- Chief Bogo
- Benjamin Clawhauser
- Duke Weaselton
- Finnick
- Banana

Second Chance Antiques (pages 12-13)
- Giggle McDimples
- Ducky
- Gabby Gabby
- Duke Caboom
- Bo Peep

Monsters, Inc. (pages 14-15)
- Randall Boggs
- Henry J. Waternoose
- Eyeglasses
- Clock
- Two-headed monster

Municiburg (pages 16-17)
- Frozone
- Violet
- Dash
- Steering wheel
- Purse

Coral Reef (pages 18-19)
- Marlin
- Dory
- Bruce
- Chum
- Anchor

New Orleans (pages 20-21)

- Big Daddy
- Eudora
- Newspaper
- Louis
- Trombone

Pride Rock (pages 22-23)

- Zazu
- Rafiki
- Nala
- Monkey standing on a rock
- Hippo's tooth

The Circus (pages 24-25)

- Ostrich
- Zebra
- Purple balloon
- Pink flower
- Yellow star

Tony's Restaurant (pages 26-27)

- Jock
- Trusty
- Tony
- Boy pointing
- Coin purse

London (pages 28-29)

- Perdita
- Cruella De Vil
- Jasper
- Dog bone
- Yellow ball

Agrabah (pages 30-31)

- Magic carpet
- Abu
- Rajah
- Watermelon slice
- Boy wearing red hat

Princess Aurora's Castle (pages 32-33)

- King Stefan
- Flora
- King Hubert
- Merryweather
- Turkey leg

Answers

Main characters and objects are circled in red. Extra characters and objects to search for are circled in green.

Motunui (pages 6–7)

China (pages 8–9)

Zootopia (pages 10–11)

Second Chance Antiques (pages 12–13)

Monsters, Inc. (pages 14–15)

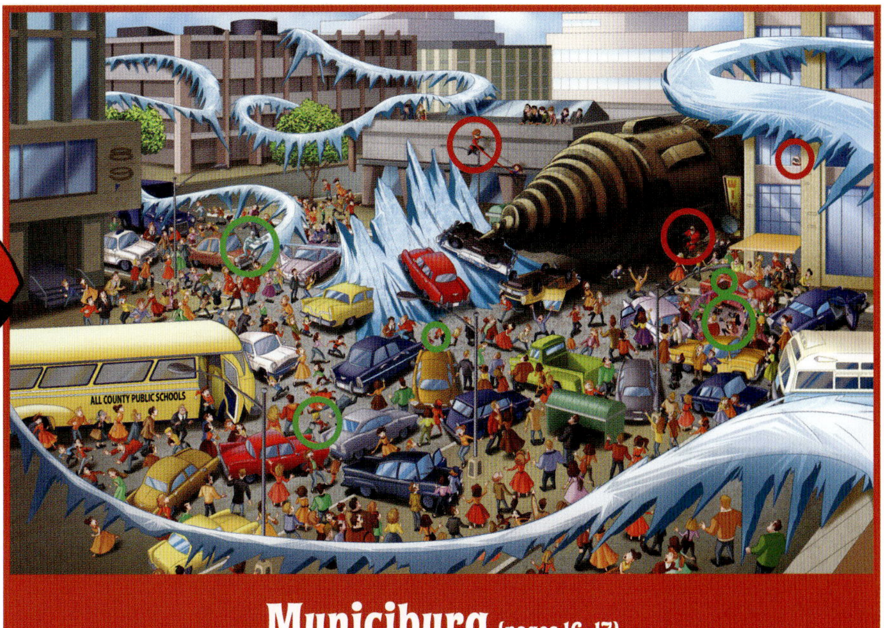

Municiburg (pages 16–17)

Coral Reef (pages 18-19)

New Orleans (pages 20-21)

Pride Rock (pages 22-23)

The Circus (pages 24-25)

Tony's Restaurant (pages 26-27)

London (pages 28-29)

Agrabah (pages 30-31)

Princess Aurora's Castle (pages 32-33)